If I Could Drive, Mama

Cari Best

Pictures by Simone Shin

xz
B

Margaret Ferguson Books

FARRAR STRAUS GIROUX • NEW YORK

For Leo and Ivy and Max —C.B.

For Mom —S.S.

Color separations by Embassy Graphics Ltd.
Printed in China by Toppan Leefung Printing Ltd.,
Dongguan City, Guangdong Province
Designed by Kristie Radwilowicz
First edition, 2016
1 3 5 7 9 10 8 6 4 2

mackids.com

Library of Congress Cataloging-in-Publication Data

Names: Best, Cari, author. | Shin, Simone, illustrator.
Title: If I could drive, Mama / Cari Best ; pictures by Simone Shin.
Description: First edition. | New York : Farrar Straus Giroux, 2016. |
    "Margaret Ferguson Books." | Summary: "A boy turns a cardboard box into a
    car and imagines what it would be like to take his mama for a drive all
    around town"—provided by publisher.
Identifiers: LCCN 2015030873 | ISBN 9780374302054 (hardback)
Subjects: | CYAC: Automobile driving—Fiction. | Imagination—Fiction. |
    Boxes—Fiction. | Mother and child—Fiction. | BISAC: JUVENILE FICTION /
    Transportation / Cars & Trucks. | JUVENILE FICTION / Imagination & Play.
Classification: LLC PZ7.B46575 If 2016 | DDC [E]—dc23
LC record available at http://lccn.loc.gov/2015030873

Our books may be purchased in bulk for promotional, educational, or business use. Please contact
your local bookseller or the Macmillan Corporate and Premium Sales Department
at (800) 221-7945 ext. 5442 or by e-mail at MacmillanSpecialMarkets@macmillan.com.

If I could drive, Mama, you would be the first passenger in my brand-new car.

I say, "It's the zippiest car in the whole world!"

And you say, "I am ready to have a ride!"

I adjust the mirror, check to see if we have gas (we do!), and turn on the radio. "Buckle up, Mama!" I say.

And you say, "I'm on it, Charlie. Did you just hear the CLICK?"

Then off we go down the road—

REV
REV
VROOM

—just you and me in
my brand-new car.

When you drive, you have to be careful of dogs and cats and

double-parked trucks—BEEP BEEP BEEP—
and other things in the way,

like street cleaners.

Our first stop is . . .

. . . Pretty Please, where you get your nails polished by
me—Mr. Charlie. I pick periwinkle for your toes and you
pick fuchsia for your fingers.

When everything is dry I say, "How do you like them?"
And you say, "I feel like Princess Mama!"

Back in the car we sing "The Wheels on the Bus" because it's our favorite traveling song.

But only you do the motions since both *my* hands have to be on the steering wheel. When the song is over I say, "We're almost there, Mama."

And you say, "Almost where, Charlie?"

But I don't want to tell you, because it's a big surprise. Then we're there . . .

. . . at the library, that's where!
I say, "I can't wait to see the new books."
And you say, "I'm going to take home three!"

I read you a story about a baby whale, and you read me one about three mischievous rabbits.

Then I say, "It's music time!"
And you say, "Can I be the one to
choose the song?"
Then we shake our sillies out . . .

. . . until I say, "It's time to go shopping!"
And you say, "Mamas *love* to shop!"

So I unlock the car with a twist of my
key and—REV REV VROOM—
we go zipping around the corner to . . .

. . . Daisy's Dress Shop, where they have the nicest dresses. And they're all exactly your size!

I say, "Which one would you like?"

And you say, "The one with pink and green."

"That's my favorite, too!" I say. "You can wear it to Charlie's Diner, which is where we are going for lunch."

The parking lot is full, so we have to wait for a space. I leave my blinkers blinking—
BLINK BLINK BLINK—until I see an empty space. Then I zoom right in! ZOOM!
Who do you think we see at the diner?

Daddy! That's who!

"Hi, guys," he says. When he sees my brand-new car, he says, "I didn't know you could drive, Charlie."

And I say, "I've been practicing."

We have delicious PB&Js with extra pickles for everyone.
And applesauce with chunks of pineapple for dessert.
After lunch you change into play clothes and I take
you—REV REV VROOM—to . . .

. . . Playground Park. But once we get there,
we ride over a rock in the middle of the road—
THUMP THUMP SQUEEEAL!

"Uh-oh!" I say when I get out to
inspect. "Not one but *two* flat tires!"
And you say, "Oh no, Charlie!"

Then I say, "Don't worry, Mama. I have my trusty tire pump in the trunk."
And you say, "I think the brakes are squeaky, too."
So I put air in the tires and squirt oil on the brakes to keep them quiet. There!
Then—REV REV VROOM—we continue on to . . .

. . . the swings where I park the car under a shady tree. I push you medium high, but when it's my turn I swing myself. My feet almost touch the sky—and I can see Jerry's Ice Cream Wagon coming down the street!

I buy creamy strawberry for you
and nutty pistachio for me.
"Yummy in my tummy!" I say.
And you say, "You took the words
right out of my mouth!"

Then—REV REV VROOM—
we are off to someplace else!

There are bumps.

There are hills.

There are red lights
that tell us to stop.

But then there is something that
makes us stop for so long that I have
to turn off the engine. MOORv.

A construction site!

I say, "This could take a while, Mama."

And you say, "How about we play a game?"

So we play I Spy to make the time go faster. And it does!

Soon the traffic person flips the stop sign to the slow
sign and finally we can *go*—REV REV VROOM—

just you and me in my
brand-new car, to the . . .

. . . neighborhood blue-water pool! We jump in together: SPLASH! It feels good to cool off after so much driving!

Then, just like that, the sun goes away and it starts to rain. Not to worry!
I turn on the wipers in my brand-new car—SWISH SWASH SWISH—
and everything is okay again. But when I look over, you seem a little droopy.

So I say, "I think it's about time for your nap, Mama."

And you say, "I don't want a nap!"

So I say, "I know! There is one more place we can go since you have been
so good. You're going to love it." REV REV VROOM—

it's the Flower Farm! I pick the
prettiest bouquet of zinnias for you,

which you hold on your lap all the
way home, trying not to fall asleep.

Then, while I'm tucking you in for your nap, you say,
"Charlie, I've had the best day ever!"
And I say, "Me, too, Princess Mama."

When you fall asleep,

I get out my bucket and soap and sponges to wash my
zippy new car—SCRUB SCRUB SCRUB—

so it will be clean and sparkly when you wake
up and we take the last trip of the day—

REV

REV

VROOM!

—to the aquarium!